Safe With Me, Baby

A Yeah, Baby Novella

FIONA DAVENPORT

Copyright

Edited by PREMA Editing
Cover design by Elle Christensen

Chapter 1

Calista

"Everything's set for your meeting at Gray Security tomorrow morning."

I heaved a deep sigh of relief, feeling like a weight had been lifted from my shoulders. The last few months had been beyond difficult for me, ever since I'd gotten shot while on a mission in a country where my body would never have been claimed if my wound had killed me. The agency wasn't supposed to have been running an op there, not without looping in their government since we were allies. I knew the risks going in—knew what the lack of backup could mean for me—but it needed to be done, and I was the best person for the job.

I'd barely managed to get out of there alive, but I'd done it and brought the intel we needed with me. It cost me a few weeks in the hospital, months of rehab, and ultimately my career since the incident played a large part in my decision to leave the CIA. Even with all that, I had no regrets. What I'd done had saved countless lives, and it was time to move on with my own.

"Thanks, Evie. I appreciate your help on this." I'd turned to Genevieve Shaw because I knew she understood what I was going through, to a certain extent at least. I respected the hell out of her, for her skills as an operative and as the instructor she currently was.

"Cut the bullshit, Cali. You don't owe me any gratitude. We both know you could walk into any security firm in the country and land yourself a position without any assistance from me."

"Maybe," I sighed. "But there would be too many damn questions I couldn't answer. Most of the shit I've done for the agency is classified. My records have more lines blacked out than not."

"You can still take me up on my offer. Say yes, and I'll call Alex right now. You could fly back tonight and start tomorrow." Her voice was cajoling as she tried to talk me into training the newbies with her.

I had no doubt she was right. If she called him, her husband would absolutely offer me a position as a trainer. "Only because you can talk your hubby into just about anything."

"We'd be lucky to have you."

"And so will Gray Security." My tone brooked no argument as I walked into a bar down the street from the hotel I'd checked into when I'd landed in Atlanta a few hours ago. Although it appeared to anyone watching me that my focus was wholly on my phone conversation, I took in every minute detail as my eyes scanned the bar.

"Fine," she huffed. "But if you change your mind, give me a call."

She hung up before I could say anything else, and it made me laugh softly to myself as I walked up to the bar and claimed a stool at the end where it angled so my back was to a wall and I had a clear view of the room. My position gave me a better view of the other patrons sitting at the bar. When my gaze landed on the guy closest to me, my entire being focused completely on him.

I tried not to stare at the mouthwatering man who was drinking a beer while watching a baseball game on the big screen hung high up on the wall. Everything about him screamed sensuality—from his dark, wavy hair to his equally dark eyes and a mouth with firm, plump lips that made a woman think about kissing the fuck out of him.

He had a dangerous air about him, even while he was just sitting there. I'd noticed it when I'd only seen him from behind. He was hard to miss with those broad shoulders, lean hips and long legs stretched in front of him. It wasn't something that bothered me since I was used to dangerous men, but my reaction to him was a surprise since it was so strong. I'd never reacted to a man like this before. Then he turned towards me, and his hooded gaze struck me. Hard.

His dark eyes trailed over my face, hair, and breasts. It started out as a lazy perusal, but by the time he was done something had changed. It was intense, and I found myself wondering what it would be like to have him staring at me the same way while we were in bed together. His lips tilted up at the edges, in a smug grin that told me he had a good idea of exactly what I was thinking.

Luckily, the bartender stepped in front of us, cutting me off from his view. It gave me a moment to pull myself together. It was unsettling knowing that I needed it since I was known for my ability to remain calm under fire. Yet, somehow this stranger had the ability to get to me.

"What can I get you, sugar?"

The bartender's drawl, combined with his good looks, probably got him quite a bit of attention from women while he was working, but it didn't do a damn thing for me.

"A shot of tequila"—my gaze darted over his shoulder to the shelves lining the wall, scanning them until I found what I wanted—"the DeLeon. Follow it up with a margarita on the rocks using the Tres Agaves Añejo. Salt on the rim. And don't call me sugar or you'll end up with my very high heeled boot in your ass."

"It sounds like I underestimated you." The bartender's eyes filled with masculine approval before he turned to get my shot.

In the short time it took for him to grab the shot glass and bottle, Mr. Dangerous made his move, sliding into the seat next to mine. "Put 'em on my tab," he instructed as the bartender set my shot in front of me.

"Sure." The bartender's disappointment was clear in his voice and with the way he stiffly walked away to make my margarita.

I didn't say a word, instead opting to sip at my DeLeon. I savored the lightly sweet vanilla and roasted agave flavor, balanced out by a touch of black pepper.

"No salt and lime to go with your shot?"

"It isn't that kind of tequila. Something you'll discover when you see the bill."

His eyes heated, and he didn't seem to care how much he'd just dropped on my drinks. "So no body shots, then?"

I shook my head in the negative, but my tongue swept across my lips at the thought of licking salt off his skin.

"Such a shame."

His husky tone sent shivers along my spine. He was even more dangerous than I'd originally thought, and I was damn lucky not to have met him in a professional capacity while I was with the agency. If I had, I wouldn't have been able to consider giving in to the temptation he presented.

"Have a taste?" I offered him the glass with a small smile.

His fingers slid against mine as he took it from me. When he lifted it to his mouth, he twisted his wrist so he could drink from the same place where my lips had rested before his.

"Mmm. Sweet and spicy," he murmured.

With the way he was looking at me, it was obvious that he was talking about more than the tequila. He moved with a subtle slide of his upper body, gliding a little closer to me when the bartender returned with my margarita and a black folder that he set in front of the man next to me. Mr. Dangerous flipped it open, chuckling deeply when he read the total, and slid his credit card out of his wallet to place it inside.

"You weren't kidding when you said it wasn't that kind of tequila."

I was even more impressed when that was all he had to say about my expensive taste in alcohol. "I don't make jokes very often."

"That's a shame, too." He bent low and flicked his tongue at the salt on the rim of my margarita. "But what's worse is that you haven't told me your name yet."

I took a gulp of my margarita, enjoying the way his eyes heated while he watched me lick the rim of my glass right next to where he'd done so. "Since I'm currently between jobs, I should properly thank you for saving me from my bar bill."

"Come work for me."

He was crazy hot, but apparently also just plain old crazy. "You don't even know my name, or the kind of work I'm capable of doing."

He lifted a brow arrogantly. "Give me your name, and we'll solve the first problem."

"Calista," I replied with a soft laugh. "But that doesn't fix the second issue."

"Leave that to me. I'm the boss, so I'll figure it out."

"Is that what you want me to call you? Boss?"

"Fuck," he groaned, leaning closer to me and setting his arm on the back of my stool. "That sounds good coming from your pretty little mouth."

"Then I guess it's too bad for you that I already have a quasi-interview for a job I'm guaranteed to be offered tomorrow morning."

His hand slid up my back until he was gripping my neck. "Maybe we can find other occasions for you to call me boss then."

"Aren't you supposed to buy a girl dinner first?"

"You hungry?"

"Famished."

But for more than just food. It was why I let him lead me out of the bar once I finished my margarita. Why I followed him to an amazing steakhouse but barely tasted the food. And why I invited him up to my room when he was seeing me safely back to my hotel after dinner.

"You sure you want me to come in?" He dropped his forehead to mine, his nose sliding against mine briefly as he backed me against the door.

"Yes."

He moved an inch closer, my pebbled nipples brushing against his chest. "You know what's going to happen if I go in there with you, baby," he breathed against my lips.

With my hand behind my back, I slid my keycard into the lock and twisted the handle. We tumbled into the room as the door opened, and he kicked it shut behind us. With his arms wrapped around me and his mouth devouring mine, we staggered to the bed and crashed down onto the mattress in a tangle of limbs. We ripped at each other's clothes, buttons flying everywhere. I enjoyed the feel of his skin under my hands, his hard muscles bunching as he moved.

I only had half a second to appreciate him, but that's all I needed to see that he was fucking gorgeous. Words written in calligraphy were tattooed across the top of his chest, and along one on his ribs underneath his left pec. Both nipples were pierced with small silver rings, and I wondered just how he would react if I were to suck one into my mouth.

I lost my train of thought, my nails digging into his shoulders as his mouth took mine, hard and long in a delicious kiss. With those sweeps of his tongue and nibbles of my lips, he built the need inside me. I was practically squirming with it when his mouth left mine and moved down to my right breast. He was rough, giving me the edge of his teeth and then soothing the sting with his tongue. His fingers tugged hard at my other nipple, sending streaks of fire straight to my core.

He built the fire inside me until I was pleading with him to take me. "Please."

"Not yet, baby. I want to make this last. Once I get inside of you, it's going to be so fucking hard to hold off."

His head moved lower, his body shifting down the bed. My thighs parted for him, and he pushed my legs over his shoulders. I tried to move them away, feeling too exposed to him, but he gripped them in his strong hands and held me there.

"Let me, baby. I need to taste you."

"Okay, boss," I breathed out, earning me a raspy chuckle against my core as he cupped my ass and lifted me off the mattress and straight to his mouth.

"I told you I'd find other reasons for you to call me boss."

If he was any other man and I was in any other position, I would have kicked his ass for that. Instead, I lifted my hips higher, making it easier for him to devour me. And that's exactly what he did. With the first swipe of his tongue against me, I was lost.

He growled low in his throat as he fed from me. He used his tongue to suckle me before stabbing deep inside me. I writhed, my fingers clenched in the sheets while he built me higher and higher. Then he added a finger, and my orgasm crashed over me.

"Fuuuck," I screamed.

"Yes," he hissed out. "That's what I intend to do. Fuck your tight little pussy until neither of us can take it anymore." Then he was gone, sliding his body up and over mine, wedged between my legs. The shadow along his jaw scraped against my skin before he knelt up and positioned his cock against my entrance.

He pushed in, just an inch, and stopped. "Please," I gasped, jerking my hips up in an attempt to drive him further inside me.

"I love hearing you say please like that, your voice filled with a need only I can fill.

But I'm going to love the feel of your tight little pussy around my cock even more."

He withdrew, his dark eyes on mine, and then he pushed forward again.

Slowly.

"Please."

Gently.

"More."

Inch by inch.

"Fuck me!"

My body resisted his invasion as his thick length stretched me. But even as I felt the sting, I also felt empty without him. I was slick with my need, writhing beneath him as my pussy clamped down against him. He rocked his hips, withdrawing partially before giving me what I'd asked for—what I so desperately needed. His mouth crashed down against mine, swallowing my scream as he drove hard and buried himself in me to the hilt.

"Mine," he growled into my mouth.

My legs slid around his hips, pulling him tighter and holding him in place. He remained still for a little bit, giving me time to get accustomed to his size.

"Breathe, baby."

"You're so big."

"And you're so fucking tight." Of course I was. It'd been forever since my one failed experiment at sex—not something I wanted to admit to, or even think about, while he was inside me.

"You ready for more?"

I swiveled my hips and nodded.

"Thank fuck," he groaned. "Because I'm not going to last long and I want you to come with me."

He began to thrust, with hard and deep pumps of his hips. Each drive of his body jolted mine against the mattress, but with his big hands pinning my hips in place, I took each stroke as he gave it to me.

"I'm close," I panted.

He used his thumb, circling my clit and throwing me over the edge. My pussy clamped down on his cock, squeezing him as he slammed home a few more times before planting himself deep and exploding inside me.

"That was fucking amazing." His voice was raspy as we both tried to catch our breath.

"Mmm," I agreed, unable to form actual words at that point. I trailed my fingers along his chest and arms, tracing the ink I found there.

His fingers did some exploring of their own, eventually coming to rest on the scar on my belly from my recent bullet wound. "What's this from?"

"It's a long story." One I didn't want to—and couldn't—really explain.

"I've got all the time in the world for you."

I liked the sound of that, a little too much. Sliding my hand lower, I stroked his length which was already hardening again. "How about we use that time a different way?"

"I'll let you get away with that. But only for now, baby," he whispered against my lips.

"Whatever you say, boss," I quipped back.

It worked as the perfect distraction, as he went about showing me why he was the boss in bed. Afterwards, lying in his arms as the sun started to peek through the curtains, I felt energized even though I'd barely gotten any sleep. It fucking sucked that I couldn't stay like this forever, but I had shit to do if I wanted to get my new life started. And after this night, I had one hell of a reason to want to stay in Atlanta.

Chapter 2

Xander

"Jessa!" I sifted through the mess of folders on my desk and prayed for patience. I had an intercom but yelling released some of the stress. Hopefully, it would keep me from a rash reaction like firing her. "I need the paperwork for my next appointment." I couldn't find it in the pile, so I shoved everything to the opposite end of my large, corner desk. Another task I'd have to ask her to re-do. Everything was running at a snail's pace since I hired Jessa, but she was a sweet kid and I could tell she was trying.

I didn't normally have a softer side. In fact, I was known for being rigid and uncompromising, pretty much a total asshole. But, I had my moments and one of them was when my assistant, Margaret, an extremely efficient and sarcastically funny woman in her sixties, had announced she was retiring. She'd asked me to hire her eighteen-year-old granddaughter because she was too sheltered and needed to get some experience in the real world. Margaret said she would stay on and help her out until she got the hang of things, so I agreed. Then Margaret's appendix had burst, and she was currently in the hospital. Leaving me with no one but the teenager with her head in the clouds.

In the rarest of occurrences, I happened to have one of those moments the night before as well.

Calista.

Something about that woman inspired some softness, although parts of me were certainly rigid. I had a completely foreign desire to possess another person. I wanted to throw her over my shoulder, take her home, and tie her to my fucking bed so I didn't have to share her with anyone else. With her long, inky black hair, high cheekbones and full lips she had a face Hollywood would love. She was tall, which I appreciated because even though I was still quite a few inches taller, I didn't have to bend in fucking half to kiss her. Her body was lean and toned, with endless legs that had shown off her strength when they clenched around me as I fucked her tight, little pussy. Last night had been the greatest fucking sex I'd ever had in my life.

Shit. I had an interview in less than twenty minutes, and I was hard as a fucking rock. I'd probably scare the fuck out of Jessa if she saw me at that moment. I tried to think of something other than how it had felt to be inside Calista.

Baseball stats. Weston. Rhys. Thank fuck thinking about my best friends was working, and I was starting to soften. But damn it, I still couldn't stop thinking about her. When Weston and Rhys had fallen for their wives, I'd rolled my eyes and told them to stop being such pussies. And, it only took a minute of staring into her dark brown eyes to know exactly what they'd been talking about. There was no doubt in my mind that this woman fucking belonged to *me*. Not that I'd be admitting it to either of those jackasses any time soon.

A knock on my door broke through my thoughts, and Jessa stood there timidly, holding a file. "I'm sorry," she practically squeaked. "I forgot to bring it in with the other folders." I tamped down the urge to shout that it was probably a good thing or it would be lost in the pile behind me. She'd organized client folders all morning, then brought them in and set the unsteady pile on my desk. I asked her to move them and start putting them in the filing cabinet but just as she was reaching for them, my phone rang and she sprang to answer it, knocking the pile and sending everything flying in all directions. She'd started crying and fled the room.

I sighed, I didn't need to bring down the wrath of Margaret on my head, so I just moved everything and tried to get ready for my appointment. "Thank you," I grated, holding back my temper. The point was that she was trying, right? She handed me the file and spun around, scurrying from the office.

Flipping it open, I scanned the CV of C. Lewis. I'd recently picked up a handful of high-security clients, and it required hiring more bodyguards so we wouldn't be short-staffed. This guy had been recommended by a friend from the agency who Weston had introduced me to. Evie Shaw was one of the most badass women I knew and if she had a hand in training this guy, I wanted him.

There was a whole shitload of

"classified" typed on the papers when it came to work experience. My security clearance was higher than most people knew. Even Weston, who was currently CIA, didn't know just how deep I was in with the agency. I'd been secret service when I first started out and had risen through the ranks at lightning speed. I realized quickly that I would be happier answering to myself, but I'd made the right contacts. They came to me for help on certain cases and returned the favor when needed.

Digging into his missions was as simple as picking up the phone, and they'd sent the un-redacted file over, but it wasn't really necessary. All I'd needed to consider the guy was the recommendation of someone in the agency that I trusted implicitly. This interview was more of a formality than anything as I fully intended to hire the guy.

"Mr. Gray." Jessa's high-pitched voice pierced the silence in the room through the intercom. "You have a visitor."

"You mean my appointment?" I asked after pressing the little button on the box.

"Um, I think—maybe? I—let me double check—"

Fucking hell. "Just send them in,

Jessa."

My door opened and in walked the star of all my daydreams. "Calista," I greeted with surprise, jumping to my feet and rounding the desk. I could feel the grin splitting my face, insanely happy that she hadn't been able to stay away from me. Her mouth formed a cute O, like she was shocked about something. Had she expected me to be upset that she'd showed up at my office. Clearly, I needed to prove that wasn't the case. Before she could say anything, I slammed my door shut and pushed her up against it, my mouth crashing down on her.

By the way my heart was racing and my blood pumping, you'd think I hadn't kissed her in years instead of hours. She tasted so fucking good, like peppermint and something that was all her own. My tongue danced with hers, and my hips involuntarily rolled into her when she moaned. Before I fucked her against the door to my office, I tore my mouth from hers and buried my face in her neck. Her chest rose and fell rapidly as she panted, and I fought the instinct to feel the beat of her heart by palming her tits.

"Baby, I didn't expect to see you today. I'm so fucking glad you're here, but I have an appointment any minute. Can you come back in about an hour? I'll have you for lunch." *No, that was not a slip of the tongue.*

"I don't think that's a good idea," she mumbled. I pulled back and inspected her beautiful face, trying to decipher what had changed between leaving her in the morning and right that moment.

"Did something happen with your interview?" If it hadn't gone well, I was going to do everything in my power to get her to come work for me. Jessa could help out one of my managers and Calista could help me. My only requirement would be that she bring me my lunch every day and spread it across my desk. The picture of eating her pussy while she was sprawled there in front of me almost broke my control. But, I was a fucking professional, and I needed to handle the interview first.

"I haven't had the appointment yet." Her eyes darted around the office, looking at everything but me. My eyes narrowed, and I grabbed her chin, forcing her to meet my gaze.

"Calista, what's going on?"

"My interview is at Gray Security, Xander." Her dark eyes were studying me closely.

Then everything clicked, and I let go of her to run my hands through my hair. "You're C. Lewis?" She nodded. "Holy fuck," I whispered, her file running through my photographic memory. I felt ten years of my life immediately fall away. Right then and there I vowed, never again would she be in that much fucking danger. I didn't care how capable she was. I was going to hire her and keep her close so I could protect her.

Besides, once we got married and had kids, she'd have to quit this line of work anyway.

That thought brought me up short. That was fucking fast. I mentally shrugged; that didn't make it untrue. Then I remembered. We might just be well on our way there since we hadn't used a condom the night before.

"I guess I'll be moving back to D.C.," she sighed.

"What the fuck are you talking about?" I growled.

"I can't stay here without a job, Xander. Evie offered me a position—"

"Hell to the motherfucking no, baby. You are not going anywhere. You have a job; I'm hiring you. I'd been intending to offer you the job before I knew it was you."

She scoffed, "I can't work for you, Xander."

"Why the fuck not?" I was seriously considering bending her over my knee and spanking her ass until it was cherry red.

"It's one thing to joke around about me calling you boss in bed, but it's another thing entirely for you to be my actual boss. We slept together, and the attraction between us is still there. It would make it incredibly difficult for us to work together. The barn door is already open so to speak, and leaving it as a one-night stand won't close it."

I closed my eyes and pinched the bridge of my nose. *And this day had started out so well...*

Chapter 3

Calista

I had a reputation for being unflappable in the field. Nothing ever threw me for a loop. But when I walked through the door to the office and found Xander on the other side of it, I was stunned. In an instant, I went from excited anticipation for the position I was about to take, to crushing disappointment. There was no way in hell I could work for Xander after the night we'd spent together. There went the job that would allow me to stay in Atlanta and see what could build between us. And judging from the look on his gorgeous face, I was going to have a hell of a time convincing Xander how obvious it was that I couldn't take the job.

"I don't mix business and pleasure."

"Don't," he growled, his dark eyes popping open and meeting mine with a burning intensity that had me taking a step backwards.

I didn't have anywhere to go, though, since the closed door was right behind me. "Xander," I whispered, my sadness over the situation in which we found ourselves filling my voice.

"No," he barked. "I'm not going to stand here and listen to you boil us down to less than what we really are."

Even though my heart raced at the way his voice got raspy, I couldn't let it sway me. "It was one night—" I started, but he didn't let me finish my thought.

"Enough of your one-night bullshit," he hissed, pinning me to the door with his hard body while his hands pressed against it on either side of my head. "It was the first night of many—something which we were both on the same page about when we parted ways this morning, damn it."

I dropped my head onto his chest. "That was before I walked in here and discovered you were the guy I was interviewing with."

"That's an excuse, and I'm not willing to accept it. Nothing's really changed."

My head snapped back up, and my spine straightened. If he was trying to go about convincing me to take the job and keep him in my bed, he was doing a shitty job of it. Pissing me off was definitely not the way to go. “It’s not an excuse,” I spat out. “It’s the reality of our situation.”

“Our reality is that you’re going to damn well learn how to mix business and pleasure because you’re going to spend your days working with me and your nights in my bed.”

“You can’t force me to take the job!”

His eyes narrowed, and his jaw hardened with determination. “Fight me for it.”

“What?” I sputtered, my hands pushing at his chest while I tried to figure out what the hell he was getting at.

“You heard me. You win, you don’t have to take the job. But if I win, you’re going to work here, and I don’t want to hear any more bullshit about us being a one-night stand.”

His voice rang with confidence—too fucking much of it. I was a woman in a man’s world, which meant I was used to being underestimated on a regular basis. It had irritated me in the past, but it hurt like hell to think Xander believed it would be easy to defeat me on the mat. “You might want to think twice before you challenge me. Many others have done it before you, assuming I’d be an easy target. They learned the hard way, each and every time, exactly how stupid they were. I'm just that damn good."

He jerked a thumb over his shoulder, aiming towards his desk. "Based on the sheer volume of redacted information in your file, I'm expecting you to be incredibly skilled."

I was uncomfortable thinking about him reading my file, even the little information they would have given him access to. After the way we met, the night we'd spent together, I didn't see Xander as a colleague. He was the man I wanted to date, and I wanted him to look at me the same way. But at the same time, I also didn't want him to see me as anything less than his equal. His willingness to put our potential future together on the line made me wonder if he really did, though. "Then why the challenge?"

"Because I'm that fucking good, too. And my motivation will give me the edge."

That was a damn good answer. "Okay, you're on," I conceded.

"Let's go." He grabbed my hand and yanked me away from the door to open it.

When he led me past his receptionist, she let out a frightened squeak and almost fell off her chair. He barely paid any attention to her, except for the irritated frown he sent her way. “You make some interesting hiring choices.”

“You’re a choice. Her? Not so much,” he chuckled. “Her grandmother talked me into it. Now I’m stuck with Jessa, who’s received no training at all, while Margaret recovers from surgery.”

Based on what Evie had shared with me about Gray Security, I expected the owner to be a hardass. But knowing Xander had a soft side just made him even more attractive. Damn it, why did it have to be him behind that damn door?

“Where are you taking me?” I asked grumpily.

“Here,” he replied as he led me into a large room that had been set up as a gym, shutting the door behind us and locking it.

“I’m not dressed for sparring.” I gestured down at the pantsuit and stiletto heels I’d chosen to wear for my interview.

“Neither am I,” he pointed out as he kicked off his shoes and jerked his suit jacket off.

I copied his actions, but I paused when I looked up and found him bare-chested. His nipple rings glinted in the overhead lighting and his tattoos rippled with every movement of his muscles. “This isn’t naked wrestling.”

He slid his belt out of his pant loops and tossed it onto the floor in the corner where the rest of his clothes were piled. "Remind me to suggest that sometime in the future. Sounds like fun."

"Xander," I growled.

"I only took off the stuff that restricted my movements. I'll leave my pants on." His gaze slid over my body. "For now."

"Cocky bastard," I muttered as I walked over to the center of the mat.

"Ready?" he asked as he joined me, dropping into a fighting stance.

Moving my arms into position and bending my legs, I motioned him forward with a wave of my fingers. As he stepped towards me, I forced myself to view him as an opponent while I went into combat mode. I held my position, waiting for him to strike first, kicking out at his left leg as I side-stepped his first punch. Swiveling on the balls of my feet, I quickly turned and aimed a hit at his kidney, but he was ready for me and blocked it. He followed it up with a quick jab to my stomach, and air burst past my lips involuntarily. Then he moved in close, tossing me onto the mat hard. As quickly as I could, I flipped up and back onto my feet.

From what I'd seen so far, he was as incredible as he claimed to be and he wasn't holding much back. It was an odd time for it, but knowing he was giving it everything he had made me grin even as I kicked up at his middle, bending low right after I connected to attempt a sweep of his legs. He anticipated my move, sending me to the ground again using my momentum against me.

Scrambling up, I ripped my blouse over my head. It was restricting my movements, just like his shirt would have, and it also gave me a slight advantage for that brief moment when he couldn't resist staring at my breasts wrapped in the lacy pink bra I'd picked out while thinking of him. It was all the time I needed to jump in the air, landing a flying kick with both legs to his chest. I followed him down to the mat, intending to land on top of him with my arm against his throat. I must have given it away somehow, because he quickly rolled me underneath him and pinned me to the mat with both arms above my head and my legs held down by his powerful thighs.

"Concede," he breathed into my ear as I struggled beneath him.

"You're good." It was all I was willing to give at the moment, even though he'd won fair and square. A small part of me couldn't help but wonder if I'd fought as hard as I could, or if I'd held back because I really did want to work for him, even if it complicated things.

"I'll show you just how fucking good I am."

We went from fight to fuck mode in a blink of an eye. He tore my pants down my legs while I ripped the zipper down on his to free his cock from its constraints. His fingers slid up my thigh, going straight for my pussy and he groaned when he found how wet I was. Wrapping my hand around his cock, I gave him a couple of quick strokes. "I want you inside me. Now."

His eyes darkened with need, and he slammed his mouth down on me to claim it in a brutal kiss. As I wrapped my legs around his waist, his cock nudged my entrance. With one powerful thrust, he drove deep inside me. My head fell back against the mat, and he shifted forward, his mouth following mine. Refusing to end the kiss while he hammered in and out of my body. He plunged his tongue into my mouth and stroked mine, holding my head steady with a hand gripped tightly in my hair.

His other hand moved to my tit, plucking at the nipple before sliding further down to circle my clit. He swallowed my cries of pleasure, my orgasm building hard and fast. I leaned up and sucked on one of his metal rings, loving the moan and shiver it caused. He thrust even harder and let go, my head falling back and my nails digging into his shoulders.

"You feel so fucking good, baby. Your tight little pussy fits me so perfectly." He angled his hips and pounded into me harder, finding my G-spot and throwing me over the edge. "Fuck yeah, that's what I needed. Your pussy strangling my cock while you come."

"Xander," I cried out, trembling beneath him.

He pulled back and then drove deep once more, his hips slamming against mine as he roared out his release above me. It was the hottest thing I'd ever seen, or experienced, and it had happened in the middle of my interview on the floor of his company's workout room.

"Shit," I groaned. "I didn't mean for that to happen."

"Get used to it because it's going to happen a fuck of a lot more." Xander flashed me a smug grin and pointed at the light streaming through the windows lining one wall. “It’s a new day, which means the one-night stand label doesn’t apply to us anymore—not that it ever did.”

Chapter 4

Xander

Reluctantly, I pulled out of Calista and gave her a quick kiss on the lips before hopping to my feet. Extending a hand, I grasped her fingers and pulled her up. She frowned and looked down at where my come slid down her legs, her expression quickly turning into a scowl. I tried incredibly hard, *I swear I did,* to keep the smug grin off my face. The deepening of her scowl when she looked at me made it clear I hadn't succeeded.

Unable to resist, I pecked her lips once more. "Wait here, baby." I jogged over to a table where fresh towels were stacked and snagged one, along with a bottle of water from a cooler sitting next to it. I gathered up our clothes, then returned and handed her everything before sweeping her up into my arms, ignoring her gasp of surprise. She weighed practically nothing, her body all lean muscle, and it was sexy as fuck.

"Put me down. I'm too heavy."

I laughed straight from my belly. "Baby, you weigh about as much as a pillow."

She sputtered as I stalked to an unmarked door across the room and held her tight with one arm while digging in the pocket of my pants for a key. I found it, tossed the slacks over my free arm, stuck the key in the knob, then twisted and pushed through the door.

We were in a large bathroom with travertine flooring, cream painted walls, a cream and gold swirled counter with a sink on the left end, and an enormous shower, the tiles made to match the floor. There was also a bench against the wall opposite the counter top and large mirror, and it sat next to another door. It was something of a cross between a locker room and an elegant bathroom. It was my private space, connecting my office to the gym. I set Calista on the counter, and she hissed at the cold on her heated, bare skin. I handed her the water, and she drank some as her wide eyes took in everything around her.

"This is awesome," she breathed.

I grinned. "You're welcome to use it anytime. I'll have an extra key made today."

Her brow furrowed and she shook her head. "No, no special treatment for the newbie. I need to earn my place here."

Using my thumb and index finger, I pinched her chin to keep our gazes locked. "First of all, you are the most qualified security expert I have on my team. Second"—my eyes narrowed, my voice taking on a dangerous edge—"The way I handle my employees is entirely up to me. Third, this"—I pointed back and forth between us—"is not an illicit affair. I won't hide it. You are mine, and I'm going to make sure every motherfucker in the state of Georgia knows it."

"I'll be branded as the woman who slept her way to the top!" she cried. "I've worked my ass off to earn the respect I'm given. We shouldn't even be having a relationship at all!"

I swallowed an angry retort and sighed, cupping her face and kissing her nose. As much as I hated to admit it, she had a point. About the respect thing, not the relationship because that was definitely happening. "How about a compromise? We keep this low-key, not hiding it, but not a blatant show that we're together either. And, I'll start you out with jobs I would give a rookie"—I rolled my eyes at the ridiculousness of it all—"no matter how overqualified you are. And ignoring the fact that if you were just any other guy, with your qualifications, you would have automatically jumped to the top of the seniority list."

She considered my words for a moment, the cogs of her mind almost visibly spinning. "Well, maybe not *all* the way down to rookie." I laughed and let her face go to pick up the towel I'd brought with us. "It would be a non-issue if you'd just realize that working together while fucking is a bad idea."

My head snapped up, and I glared at her. "Stop fighting what you know feels right, Calista. And, I may fuck the hell out of you at times, but we are more than temporary fuck buddies. I don't want to hear you refer to us that way again."

Irritated, I busied myself cleaning up our combined come from her legs and pussy, as well as my groin.

"Shit!" Her exclamation grabbed my attention, and I glanced around, looking for whatever it was that had upset her. But when I faced her again, she was staring at the towel. "We didn't use a condom, damn it!"

"So?"

"SO?? We may not have to worry about pregnancy, but how the hell do I know if you're clean?"

I latched onto her comment about pregnancy, but I decided to address her other concern first. "I was tested after the last time I had sex, and it was"—I fucking blushed. *Seriously?* Clearing my throat, I tried to shake it off—"four years ago."

Her jaw went slack, and her eyes widened for a beat. Then her face softened, and her mouth snapped shut. She pressed her lips together, but I didn't miss the subtle lifting of the corners.

"Um." She couldn't keep the small smile from forming once she started to speak. Her happiness at my lengthy, self-imposed celibacy made it worth it. "I'm clean too. I've only been with one—"

A deep growl rumbled in my throat as fury climbed to the surface. "Stop right there. I can't handle the thought of anyone else touching you. It makes me want to hunt the motherfucker down and cut off his dick."

She narrowed her eyes for a second, then shrugged and seemed to move past it. "Well anyway, I'm clean too."

Now, about that other thing. "What did

you mean when you said we didn't have to worry about pregnancy?"

"I'm on birth control. In my... previous line of work, it was a necessary precaution. So, I've been on a shot for years."

Fuck! That meant my hopes that I'd put my baby in her the night before were dashed. "How long does it last?"

She hopped down from the counter and started donning her underwear. "Three months."

Being prepared, having a plan, those things were in my nature, something that was an asset in my field. Which led me to the need to calculate the time I'd have to wait before it would be feasible for me to knock her up. The answer would affect the jobs I assigned her, not that I was going to share that information. No need to piss her off unnecessarily. I began to dress as well, casually asking, "When was your last shot?"

She'd been tugging on her pants, but she stopped and looked up at the ceiling as she thought. Then her expression slowly morphed into one of terrified shock. "Motherfucker!" she shouted. She frantically tugged her pants the rest of the way on and scrambled for the rest of her clothes.

"Calista," I snapped. She ignored me, so I grabbed her around the waist and slammed her bottom back down on the counter. "Why the fuck are you freaking out?"

She winced and watched me apprehensively. "I forgot to go in for my last dose." Her face turned pleading. "I'm so sorry. I was recovering from being shot, and it slipped my mind. I'll take care of it, I promise."

Why the fuck was she apologizing? Did she think I'd be upset about it? I was the total opposite, my hopes springing to the surface again. It was entirely possible I'd gotten her pregnant last night. After four rounds, I'd certainly filled her with enough of my come to make sure one of my boys stuck. Our escapade on the gym floor—"What do you mean you were shot?!" I practically shouted as my brain caught up with everything she'd said.

"Calm down, Xander." She adopted a soothing tone, but it bounced right off my wall of anger. "I'm fine. It was just a little nick."

We weren't done with that discussion, but I needed to know something else. "You'll 'take care of it' means what exactly?" I inquired.

"I'll go to the doctor and get a morning after pill and a new shot."

"The fuck you will!"

Calista's expression turned mutinous, her dark, espresso eyes narrowing. Some of her black hair had escaped the knot she'd put it in and floated around like a halo. She looked fucking gorgeous all riled up, and my cock had taken notice.

"It's really none of your business," she huffed. "I'll report tomorrow for my first day."

"It's none of—" I almost choked on my wrath, my hard on forgotten—*mostly*—and before I could get another word out, she spun around and yanked open the door to the gym, letting it slam against the wall with a loud bang.

I followed her as she streaked across the floor, but I had the feeling that I wouldn't win this argument by keeping her in the office and talking myself to death. Calista was a level-headed, unflappable person. Until it came to me, apparently. The thought made me grin, knowing I got to her. It was obvious she was also stubborn as fuck, and it would take action over words for me to win. And I. Would. Win.

Chapter 5

Calista

It was hard to believe Xander let me escape his office so easily. I'd figured he'd put up a fight, figuratively and quite possibly also literally, considering how well he'd sparred against me. Then again, the gleam in his eyes when I'd turned back to look at him through the glass doors had me thinking he had his reasons for letting me go. I had a feeling the tricky bastard thought he was going to convince me to do everything his way. The scariest thing was, I was starting to wonder if he might be right about that. I tossed and turned, worrying about it all night.

Once I'd cooled off and realized what I'd actually said, I regretted the way I'd told him it was none of his business. I couldn't believe I'd been so horrible to him. My only defense was that I'd been thrown completely off balance by the surge of fear, mixed with frustration and attraction, running through my system at that moment. Nobody had ever managed to pull such a wide range of emotions out of me the way Xander did. I was completely unaccustomed to feeling so much all at once, and I'd handled it badly. Really, fucking badly.

Heading back to his offices the next morning, I knew I owed him an apology. A fucking huge one.

Kicking off my first day at work by telling my boss I was sorry for being such a bitch to him because I completely lost my mind at the idea that he might have knocked me up wasn't exactly how I'd pictured starting my new career. Hell, the possibility of being pregnant wasn't a topic I'd ever imagined I'd have to discuss with a guy at all, and the circumstances of my current work situation only made it more complicated.

The morning after pill should be the obvious choice considering everything. And yet, somehow it wasn't. If anyone had asked me how I'd react to the idea of being pregnant a couple of months ago, the answer would have been simple because it just wasn't on my radar at all. I'd been completely focused on my career, with no plans to get involved with a guy, let alone have a baby.

Then I got shot, and everything changed. I'd been in the spy game long enough to know when it was time to get out. It was still a tough decision to make, but it had been the right one for me. It was also the choice that put me in the right place at the right time to meet Xander, and even with all the craziness from yesterday, I didn't regret what had happened between us.

As I pushed through the doors to Gray Security, it was as if I conjured him up out of my thoughts. He strode out of his office and straight towards me, with another hot guy right behind him. If I didn't know better, I'd think Xander had a Calista radar because he didn't even pause in his steps or need to change direction.

"Shit. Fuck. Damn," I mumbled to myself, spotting his assistant at her desk and another guy coming down the hallway, presumably just after finishing up in the gym since he was wearing athletic shorts, a T-shirt, and was rubbing his dark hair with a towel.

"Morning, baby," Xander greeted me, blocking everything else from my vison as his head bent low so he could drop a kiss on my lips.

"So much for not being blatant about us," I muttered, making him chuckle. He didn't seem the least bit concerned to see me glaring up at him. He just offered me a confident grin as I stepped away from him.

He gestured to the guy with him. "I don't think you've met Quinn. He's one of the best here, and he's engaged to Weston's sister, Jenna."

Evie had introduced me to Weston and Aspen when I'd been in Atlanta for a quick house hunting trip the month before I moved here. I grinned. "Ah yes, I believe Weston mentioned something about the fucker who does unspeakable things to his baby sister."

Quinn laughed. "Guilty as charged."

"Great, now you've met," Xander interrupted impatiently. "Excuse us."

Xander put his hand on my lower back and steered me toward his office. His assistant looked like she was about to have a breakdown. I took pity on her and stepped forward to say hello.

"Good morning, Jessa." I smiled at her. Her eyes skittered back and forth between Xander and me a few times before her shoulders relaxed slightly and she offered me a little grin back.

"Morning, Miss Lewis."

"Calista, please."

"Umm, okay." She shifted in her seat nervously. "I have some paperwork for you to fill out." She dug through a stack of folders on her desk, almost knocking them over before Xander grew impatient and went to the filing cabinet behind her to yank open a drawer. He pulled out a manila file and handed it to her. She shoved it towards me like she thought it was going to explode in her hands or something. "If you could get most of it back to me by tomorrow, that would be great. But I'd like the contact information this morning, if that's okay."

"Sure, but I'll have to change most of it soon since I'm going apartment hunting this weekend."

"Oh, okay. That's fine, I guess." Her gaze darted down at the folder and then back up to my face. "My grandmother lives in a great neighborhood, and the house next door to her just went up for sale. It's super convenient to work, too."

"It's sweet of you to mention it, but I don't want the hassle of a house. I'm not used to being around to do maintenance stuff because I used to travel a lot for work, so I never needed to learn how to do that stuff.

An apartment or condo will work better for me."

"There are a couple of open units in my building," the dark-haired guy offered, having made his way down the hall and into the reception area. His eyes scanned up and down my body as he offered me a cocky smile. "Or if you're looking for a roommate, you could just move in with me."

"Shut the fuck up, Reid. And go put on some real clothes, dammit," Xander growled at him. I felt his fingers wrap around my upper arm, and Jessa looked like she was about to have a panic attack as she stared at us with wide eyes. I let him lead me into his office without putting up a fight. He might have won the little battle on the mat the day before, but that didn't mean he was going to win all of them. But he didn't have to know that. Not yet, anyway.

"That's not quite how I pictured this morning going," I sighed after he shut the door behind us.

"Fuck," he groaned, running his hands through his dark hair and making it look like he'd just rolled out of bed. "This is going to be a lot harder than I thought. There's no fucking way I'm going to be able to stand by and watch as my guys flirt with you. Not even on my best day, which today most definitely isn't because I barely slept last night. It only took one damn night for me to get used to having you in my arms."

"I didn't sleep well, either," I admitted softly.

He moved behind me and wrapped his arms around me. "I should have done it."

"Done what?" I leaned against him, feeling myself relax for the first time since I walked out yesterday.

"It took everything I had in me not to break into your hotel room last night. If I'd known you needed me, I wouldn't have held back. But with the way you stormed out of here yesterday, I figured you needed a little time to adjust."

"I did," I sighed.

His arms tightened. "I understand, or at least I'm trying to. But never again, Calista. If we have a problem, we're going to hash it the fuck out right away. There won't be any going to bed angry, or without each other, in this relationship."

"I wasn't angry when I went to bed." Even though he couldn't see my face, I closed my eyes as I opened myself up to him. I might be a badass when it came to my job, but not so much when it came to being emotionally vulnerable. “It was guilt for how I reacted. For what I said to you. I’m so sorry.”

“Calista. Baby,” he sighed, turning me in his arms and cupping my jaw in his palms to turn my face up. “Open those fucking gorgeous brown eyes and look at me.”

I did as he asked, and the soft look on his face made me want to cry. “I’m not going to ask the doctor for the morning after pill,” I blurted out. “I’m going to go in and see her, though. If we’re going to keep on doing this, then I need to do something about birth control. For the future. In case I’m not already pregnant.”

“There’s no if about it, Calista. We’re definitely going to keep having sex." My lips parted, but he didn’t give me the chance to argue before he swooped down and claimed my mouth in a demanding kiss. One that left me almost breathless by the time he lifted his head again. “Often.”

“You’re too damn sexy for my own good,” I grumbled.

“I promise to make it up to you.” His dark eyes twinkled with humor. “With as many orgasms as you want.”

“I’m so fucked,” I whispered.

“You’re going to be.”

I made a mental note to stock up on condoms since we wouldn't know if I was pregnant for a couple more weeks. At the pace we were going, if he hadn't already knocked me up, he could do it a million times over before then.

Chapter 6

Xander

Sleeping without Calista had been fucking torture, and I refused to do it again. Considering her determination to be strictly professional at work, I was pretty sure I could convince her that I had the solution to both. I kissed her again, enjoying the feel of her incredible body as she melted into me. My hands traveled down to grip her ass, and I jerked her forward so there was no room between us.

When we finally came up for air, I was panting and hard as a rock. Fiery desire licked at my body, and the matching look in her eyes broke me. Kissing her again, I backed her up until she was caged between me and my desk. I grasped her waist and hoisted her onto the tabletop before sliding my hands down to her knees and opening her wide, so I could step in between. I loved how tall she was, her body fitting so perfectly with mine. I broke the kiss as my fingers danced up her blouse, making quick work of the buttons until I was able to part the fabric and marvel over the most perfect tits I'd ever seen.

Her chest was rising and falling with her rapid breaths, and it made them bounce seductively. Hooking my index fingers over the rim of the lacy, red cups, I tugged them down, revealing her rosy, peaked nipples. My mouth watered at the sight of the tight little buds.

"Xander. We can't—" Her protest turned into a moan when I wrapped my lips around one nipple and sucked in hard. Fuck, she tasted good, her honey skin almost as potent as her delicious pussy.

"I fucking love your tits, Calista," I mumbled as I let one go, only to move over to the other.

I was so fucking hard I was sure my cock would burst through the crotch of my thousand-dollar suit pants at any moment. Letting her nipple go with a pop, I groaned. "Need to be inside you, baby." Slamming my mouth down on hers again, I unbuttoned her pants and shoved a hand down, pulling aside her underwear and sinking one long finger inside her. "So fucking wet."

She moaned, her hands gripping my shoulders, fingertips digging into the muscle. I retracted my digit and brought it to my mouth, sucking it clean. It made me desperate to feel her slick walls clamping down on my cock. I practically attacked her pants, growling in frustration as I realized what a pain in the ass it was to get them off. "Skirts from now on, baby," I grunted. "Nothing but skirts. I need easy access to my woman's pussy. Underwear is optional." The thought of all those drooling idiots who worked for me getting a glimpse of what was mine had me rethinking. "Forget that. Underwear at all times unless we're at home."

I managed to get her pants and panties down her legs to puddle on the floor. She'd already undone my belt and freed my cock. I pushed her hands away after she stroked it once and her mouth turned down in a pout, her espresso eyes dulling with hurt. "If you keep touching me, I'm going to blow in your hand, and I want to be inside you when I come," I explained roughly. A sexy little smile graced her lips, and I guided her arms to hook around my neck, sighing when she plunged her hands into my hair.

Positioning myself just right, I grabbed her ass and jerked her forward as I thrust in balls deep. We both cried out, and I quickly fused our mouths together so our sounds of passion were swallowed up in each other.

Slowly, I pulled almost all the way out and pushed back in. Damn, she felt so good, her juices coating my cock so I slid in easily before her walls tightened around me, refusing to let me go. A few more slow pumps and Calista became impatient. "Harder," she demanded softly, her muscles squeezing even more. Her fingers clenched and tugged at the strands of my hair, the sparks of pleasure-pain shooting straight to the tip of my shaft.

I began to pound into her, fast, hard, and so, so deep.

"Xander! Oh yes!" Once again, I silenced her with my mouth, my tongue playing with hers, her taste an explosion of sweet honey and woman. With one hand on her ass, I kept her firmly against me, using the other to twist and pluck at her nipples. I waited until she was shaking with need before finding the hard little button between the lips of her pussy and pressing on it, causing her to scream into my mouth as she fell apart.

Putting both hands back on her sexy ass, I yanked her forward as I slammed inside, my hips pumping with wild abandon until the tingling in my spine became a rush of fire. On the next thrust, I bottomed out, shouting as my orgasm erupted and I filled her with spurt after spurt of come.

Calista's hand had slapped over my mouth, but I was sure it had been too late, and I didn't fucking care one bit. I didn't like the idea of anyone hearing my girl's sweet sounds, but I had no problem letting them know I was fucking her, marking her as mine.

"Damn it!" Calista cursed, pushing at my chest until I grudgingly moved back. She snatched up her discarded clothes and raced to the bathroom. With a sigh, I followed at a more sedate pace, taking over the task of cleaning her up when I entered. I did the same for myself and tucked my semi-hard dick back into my pants.

"We can't do that kind of thing here!" she hissed. "And, no more sex until we've got some fucking condoms."

I ignored the condom remark. I'd

pumped her so full of my come the last two days; I was sure she was pregnant. And, I had no plans to stop trying. I latched onto her former comment. "About that," I drawled. "I have a proposition for you."

She finished dressing and finger-combing her hair before she turned around and crossed her arms under her breasts, leaning back on the counter and raising an eyebrow.

"I meant it when I said I wouldn't sleep without you again." Her eyes narrowed, but she made no other outward response to my statement. "Your desire to keep our relationship professional at work is understandable. However, I don't see that happening if I don't have all of the other hours of the day to sate my craving for you. There's no guarantee that will work either, but it gives you a slightly higher chance of success."

"And, the proposal?" she prompted sassily.

I grinned at how fucking adorable the badass chick could be. "You move in with me, and I'll try to keep our relationship platonic at the office."

Calista threw her head back and laughed but stopped when she saw what I was sure was a stubborn expression on my face. “You’re serious?”

I stalked toward her, backing her into the counter and pressing my, *once again*, fully erect cock against her. “Do I feel like I’m joking, baby?” I growled.

Her eyes heated and her hips bucked so minutely, I almost missed it. She wanted to say yes. Using my mouth and tongue, I attempted to persuade her further.

Tearing her lips from mine, she took a deep breath and stared into my eyes. “I’ll think about it.”

I shrugged. “You’ve got until the end of the workday to decide,” I informed her as I ushered her back into my office. “But, one way or another, you’ll be permanently living under our roof, in our bed by tonight.”

Her jaw dropped. “What exactly am I deciding on if you’re giving me no choice?” she snapped.

“Of course you have a choice, baby.” I took her hand and led her to the door, opening it slowly. “You can decide whether to do this the hard way or the easy way.”

She glared at me, but a corner of her mouth was quirking up, making me grin because I knew I’d won.

"I've got a lunch and meetings the rest of the day, so I won't see you until tonight. I'll meet you at home by six. Jessa will get you the address."

She rolled her eyes and turned around to walk away, jumping a little when I gave her a firm smack on her perfect ass.

"It can't get back to the studio that I'm in danger, Xander."

I looked up from the file I was reading to study the new client in my office. He was a blonde, blue-eyed, boy next door type. Ewan McKendry was extremely fit and obnoxiously pretty. Which was a huge part of what made him a successful movie star. He was a decent actor, too.

"They'll put me in fucking lockup until my contract is done. Or, they'll stick me with the same fucking idiots they sent last time. I need someone who can protect me and do it under the radar."

"No problem," I assured him. "I think Quinn would be a great option."

Ewan shook his head. "No, I want a female."

I only had a handful of women working for me. I'd need to go through their files and find a match. "Okay, I'll find the right—"

"I already found her," Ewan interrupted. "I'm a client of Rhys Campbell, and he mentioned that you just hired a female security specialist who is one of the best in the business. I guess he talked to some woman he knows who used to be CIA? It's a perfect situation because she can pose as my girlfriend."

Rhys was a fucking dead man. And, Evie had just earned herself a prominent position on my shit list for a while, too.

"I'll have to check her availabil—" I started, but he cut me off again.

"We ran into each other in the hallway, and she said her schedule was free. So, set it up, okay?" He stood and reached across the desk to shake my hand, clearly done with the discussion.

My jaw clenched, and I ground my teeth together as I shook his hand. "I'll take care of it."

Ewan nodded and flashed his multimillion dollar smile, which only made me want to kick his ass, before walking out the door.

I followed his path and stepped into

the waiting area, scowling at Jessa. I would have felt sorry for the fact that she'd been in the path of my wrath later, but at that moment, I didn't give a fuck about anything but ripping my friend a new asshole.

"Get me Rhys Campbell on the phone." An evil smile curved my lips. "No, better yet, get his wife on the phone."

Chapter 7

Calista

"I hear your first client is a movie star."

I yanked the phone away from my ear for a moment to make sure it really was Evie calling. Yeah, it was her. "How in the hell did you hear about that already? I haven't even gotten the official word from Xander yet that he's going to put me on the case."

"Oh, the client is definitely yours, but I wouldn't say you've been assigned to it—more like Mr. Hollywood insisted you take it."

"Seriously, did you bug the place or something?" I glanced around the office Jessa had shown me to earlier that morning. Knowing Evie, I wouldn't put it past her, especially since her husband felt bad about my shooting since he was my superior at the time.

"Nah," she laughed. "You apparently made one hell of an impression on Xander.

He called to let me know how pissed off he was that I mentioned you when I talked to Rhys Campbell, the financial guy I told you about."

I dropped my head down onto the desk and banged it a couple of times for good measure. In the span of one day, Xander had gone from being not-so-subtle around the office by kissing me in front of his other employees to being completely obvious by calling to yell at people because I was going to be protecting a Hollywood heartthrob. At the rate he was going, he'd be hiring a skywriter to announce our relationship to the whole city tomorrow. "He did what?"

"You heard me. Mr. Hollywood uses Rhys as his financial guy, too, and that's how he got the recommendation for Gray Security. Xander is beyond pissed that the guy knew about you and pretty much demanded you provide his personal protection—while posing as his girlfriend."

"Fuck," I groaned. That had to have gone over like a lead balloon with Xander. "Ewan didn't mention the girlfriend idea or how he knew Rhys when I bumped into him in the hallway while he was on his way to his meeting with Xander."

"Luckily for me, most of his anger was directed towards Rhys. They've known each other forever, and they don't hold back any punches when they're fighting. All I got was a growly phone call, but Rhys got a call to his wife that's bound to put him in the doghouse for a little bit."

"Sounds like I'd better hold off on transferring my accounts over for Rhys to manage," I grumbled. Handing over my life savings to a guy who wasn't getting any from his wife in part because of me didn't sound like a smart move on my part.

"Nah, he might fool most people with the suits he wears, but he's just as much of a macho caveman as Alex... and Xander when it comes to you apparently," she trailed off, her voice turning up questioningly at the end.

"Yeah, about that," I sighed. "A funny thing happened after I got off the phone with you the other night. Xander was at the bar down the street from my hotel, and I bumped into him. Only I didn't know he was the owner of Gray Security at the time."

"From the way Xander was acting, it sounded like you bumped into him an awful lot."

I could practically hear her wagging her eyebrows suggestively. "Enough that he wants me to skip the apartment hunting and move in with him."

"Damn," she whistled. "He's even faster than Alex. It only took him a day to talk me into a week-long trip to Fiji, but it took two for him to convince me not to go house-hunting in D.C. so I could move in with him instead."

"Well, shit. When you compare him to Alex like that, it makes Xander's suggestion sound semi-sane." And it also made me wonder if I should just give in and tell him I'll move into his place.

"At least he knows about your career with the CIA," she pointed out drily. "The same couldn't be said for Alex or me, and look how well everything turned out for us."

Their marriage was like something out of the damn movies. They were together for four years without either one knowing the other had a secret life as a spy, until the agency assigned them different objectives on the same case. "Who would have ever thought the CIA's best snipers would settle down quite so much?"

My hand drifted down to my belly as I thought about Emmy and Ash, Evie and Alex's children. In nine months, I might be a mommy, too.

"Holy shit," I breathed out, as the reality of it all hit me.

"Calista! Are you still there?" Evie's voice snapped me out of my thoughts.

"Yeah, I'm here. I'm sorry, but I need to go. There's something I need to talk to Xander about."

I didn't wait for her to say goodbye before disconnecting the call and jumping out of my chair to race to my door. When I flung it open, Xander was standing on the other side. I yanked him inside and slammed the door shut again.

"I swear, between me thinking the offices were bugged by Evie and your ability to seek me out right when I want to talk to you, my new job could give my old one a run for its money when it comes to gathering intel."

He chuckled at my irritation, earning himself a death glare that should have had him worried but only made him smirk at me. "I didn't know you needed me since I came to talk to you about a case."

"Yeah, I already heard all about how I'm going to have to pretend I'm Ewan's girlfriend in my role as his bodyguard."

"Over my dead body." His eyes iced over as he paced back and forth. "I don't care what anyone says about the customer always being right. The fuckwad isn't going to get that close to you. I get that it would be easier for him to pretend like he doesn't have someone guarding him, but if that's what he wants, then he's going to have to work with someone else. There's no fucking way I'm going to stand by and—"

I rolled my eyes and interrupted his rant. "Yeah, yeah. I hear you. You're the boss around here, so it's completely up to you how to handle this. Although I would like to point out that I'm one of the best employees you have, so not using me because you can't handle watching me stand next to another guy sounds like a stupid, macho decision to me. But, I wanted to talk to you about something else."

"What?" he asked grumpily, dropping down onto one of the chairs in front of my desk.

"I thought about what you said, and I've decided to go the easy route."

His dark eyes lit up and his lips curved up in a pleased grin. "You're going to move in with me?"

"Yes," I sighed, holding up a hand when he went to stand up. "But we need to lay down some ground rules. The first one being no more sex at work. You're the one who suggested me moving in as a way for you to be able to treat me platonically at the office, and I expect you to put some damn effort into it to make sure you hold up your end of the deal."

"Oh, I'll always hold up my end of the deal, baby," he replied in a raspy voice. And then he winked at me!

"Xander," I growled. "Being all sexy and flirty is the opposite of platonic. It's shit like that I'm hoping to avoid while we're at work."

He held up his hands in a gesture of surrender. "Sorry! I can't help it. You're so damn hot that all the blood rushes out of my brain and into my cock whenever I'm around you."

"Which brings me to rule number two—if I'm going to live in your house, you're going to keep it well stocked with condoms, assuming I'm not already pregnant."

His expression fell in disappointment.

"I'm not saying you'll have to use them forever."

"Fine," he grunted, eyeing my belly. "But I get to be there when you take the test. You move in tonight, you sleep in my bed every night, and I reserve the right to convince you to go bare while we wait to find out that my swimmers did their job already."

"You can try all you want, but it's not going to work."

"I'm going to enjoy showing you just how wrong you are."

He got everything he wanted. He had me moved out of my hotel and into his house that night. Plus, he arranged for the moving truck with all my stuff to deliver everything there the following weekend. And, it turned out the motherfucker was right. I spent each night in his bed... after he'd wrung as many orgasms out of me as it took to get me to say he could take me bare.

Chapter 8

Xander

Sitting in a van outside the premiere for Ewan's newest movie, my eyes were glued to the monitor, specifically to his hand on my woman's lower back. If it dropped another inch lower, he was going to have to learn to live without the appendage.

Calista looked fucking gorgeous in her sleeveless, blood-red dress that hugged her body until the skirt flowed out from the knees down. Her long hair was swept up into a twist at the back of her neck, and her red-tipped feet peeked out from under the skirt as she walked, showing off sexy, glittery stilettos. I couldn't wait to rip that dress off her later that night and fuck her in nothing but those heels.

It irritated the fuck out of me that it wasn't my arm she was holding onto while looking so fuckable. I wasn't sure how the fuck she talked me into letting her take the job playing another man's girlfriend. It had been two weeks of keeping the fact that she lived with me a secret, hiding our relationship in public, all the things I'd sworn I wouldn't do. I should have put a fucking ring on her finger the day she moved in with me, I thought grumpily.

In order to survive the job, without murdering Ewan, I focused on the light at the end of the tunnel. I'd be walking into it tomorrow. We had an appointment for a blood test to determine whether Calista was pregnant. I didn't know precisely why, but my instincts were confident that it would be positive. I might have been worried about her reaction, especially since it meant a vast change in her responsibilities at Gray Security, but whenever I brought it up, her face softened and her lips tipped up into a tiny smile.

She played the game well, but in the short time since we'd met, I already knew her better than anyone and her poker face was non-existent to me. And, it was obvious, even if she hadn't recognized it yet, that she wanted this as much as I did. It was just an extra perk that she wouldn't be able to guard pretty-boy any longer.

My team had been surprised when I showed up for surveillance duty at the event. I was very selective about the jobs I handled personally and staking out in the van was a rarity. But, as the night went on and I got more and more tense at the sight of Ewan touching my woman, their knowing looks told me they'd heard the rumors about Calista and me.

I supposed it was a good thing they recognized it because when Ewan had briefly kissed Calista's lips while being interviewed by the press, they held me back from jumping out of the vehicle and knocking out several of his perfect, white teeth. Calista kept her cool like the professional she was, but I was slightly mollified by the tinge of pink on her cheeks. To the rest of the world, if they noticed it at all, it would look like she was blushing. The truth was, it was a flush from aggravation. She was not happy with his actions either.

That didn't mean I wasn't going to make damn sure she knew who she fucking belonged to when we got home.

My anger continued to boil, not at her, but at the situation. Still, it fueled my need to prove she was mine. Riding home separately only made it worse, and by the time her limo drove through the gate and up the long driveway to our home, I was bounding down the front steps. I wrenched open the car door before the driver could even exit the vehicle and bent so I could reach in and slide an arm around her waist. I dragged her out and lifted her into my arms, stalking inside without a word.

"Thanks, Pete," she yelled. Then she smacked my arm as I kicked the door shut and set her down. "That was rude, Xander."

"I don't give a fuck," I growled as I shoved her skirt up and lifted her so her legs were around my waist, pressing her back into an entry way wall. "I can't fucking handle much more of this, baby. I don't want him touching you." Grinding into her, I yanked the bodice of her dress down, and her tits spilled out. She gasped when I bit one of her hard, pink nipples. Then I kissed my way up the column of her throat and right before I took her lips, I whispered harshly, "If that fucker puts his mouth on you one more time, I'm going to make him disappear, and no one will ever find his body."

Using my hips as leverage, both of my

hands toyed with Calista's tits while my tongue plundered her mouth. But, I needed more so I gripped her ass and, never losing the connection of our kiss, I made my way to our bedroom. Once I reached the bed, I unceremoniously tossed her on to it, ripped my shirt over my head, and crawled over her on my hands and knees, caging her in.

Her fingers traced my tattoos, and she flicked each nipple ring. It was hot as fuck. I ran my hand through the valley between her breasts, over her stomach, and down to cup her pussy. "This is mine," I growled, dipping a finger under her panties and inside her before groaning. "So wet."

My patience was in short supply, and I wanted to see all of her, so I took hold of her dress where it was bunched under her tits and wrenched it hard. I only meant to pull it off but it tore right down the middle, allowing me to part the fabric and leave her naked but for her tiny black thong. I scrambled down to settle between her legs.

"Xander!" Calista gasped. "That was ex—oh, fuck!" She broke off with a cry of pleasure as I ripped her thong away and latched my lips onto her tight, swollen little clit.

I worked her through a fast, explosive orgasm, lapping at all of the juice rushing into my mouth as she came. "Mine," I grunted, barely aware that I'd reverted to a full-on Neanderthal.

Quickly, I flipped her over and tugged her up onto her hands and knees. With one hand on her throat and another cupping one breast, I straightened her so her back was against my chest. A lick around the shell of her ear made her shudder, and I bit the lobe lightly before asking, "Who do you belong to, baby?"

"I'm yours, Xander," she whimpered as she squirmed and arched her tit further into my palm.

"Damn fucking straight you're mine."

Pushing her gently back down, I practically ripped open my jeans to release my throbbing cock. The pale globes of her ass were almost glowing in the moonlight streaming in from the skylight above us. I was riveted to the sight as I gripped her hips and slammed inside her, bottoming out in one thrust. Calista cried out my name and her muscles immediately clamped down on my shaft.

"Tell me again," I demanded. She didn't answer right away and my hand rose and came down hard on one white cheek, leaving a pretty, pink handprint on the blank canvas. Calista sucked in a breath, and I waited to gauge her reaction. A shiver wracked her body, and I spanked her other cheek to see if it elicited the same response. This time, she also whimpered, the sound thick with passion. "Tell me, Calista."

"I'm yours," she panted.

Leaning over her, I palmed her tits and began to move, thrusting in and out. I twisted and plucked at her nipples, knowing how it drove her wild, but soon, the pace wasn't enough and I had to let them go. I straightened up on my knees and clasped her firmly in my hands, holding her still so I could begin to speed up, going faster and harder until I was pounding into her with wild strokes. Lifting one leg, I braced myself on the sole of my foot to change the angle, hitting the perfect spot inside her. Her cries had turned to screams, and I slapped her ass once more, loving the sound of her calling out my name.

"Mine," I shouted as my balls drew up, my cock swelling to its breaking point. "Fuck, baby! Fuck!"

Gliding a hand from her hip down to

the front of her pussy, I slammed in hard just as I pinched the sensitive nub between her legs. She screamed long and loud, before chanting my name and it threw me right over the edge with her.

When our orgasms calmed to aftershocks, I collapsed on her, staying buried deep, but careful to keep my weight from crushing her. I nipped at her neck and whispered, “Mine.”

“Ms. Lewis,” chirped the small, yellow-haired pixie in a white lab coat. “How are you today?” The embroidered pocket read, Dr. Lennon, but I had my doubts that she wasn’t a child pretending to be a grown-up. My eyes narrowed, and I opened my mouth but shut it when I felt a hard pinch on my thigh. I glanced incredulously at Calista, who was sitting on the exam table beside me.

“Did you just pinch me?” I asked quietly.

“I saw the look on your face, and you were about to say something rude,” she snapped, her voice equally low. “Don’t you think I did my homework, Xander? She looks young because she was only twenty when she graduated from medical school. As valedictorian, I might add. She's fucking brilliant, and I was lucky enough to have the connections to become a patient of hers. Now, go against all of your macho instincts and sit there quietly like a good boy. If you do, I'll give you a treat later." Her voice was smug at the end.

I leaned in close and bit her lobe, causing a tiny gasp. "You're just begging for a spanking, baby. And, you better be prepared to pay up on that treat. I suggest you start picturing my cock as your favorite sucking candy." Calista pressed her lips into a straight line, but her dark eyes twinkled with humor and lust.

"Okay, Ms. Lewis, I have a preliminary result from your urine test, but we'll take some blood to confirm and call you with the results in a few hours." She smiled brightly at her, and then her blue eyes focused on me. "Are you okay with your boyfriend being in here while we discuss your results?"

"Fiancé." Uh, it just sort of slipped out.

"Yes, he can—wait, what?" Calista sputtered at the same time. "Fiancé?"

Dr. Lennon glanced back and forth

between us for a second, then settled on me. "You're the father, I presume?"

"Father?" I shot to my feet and swept Calista up into my arms, hugging her tightly. "I fucking knew my boys would get the job done."

Calista laughed, with a slightly hysterical edge, and poked me in the shoulder. "Put me down, you lunatic." I ignored her and plopped my ass down on the exam table, keeping her in my lap. I was going to be a fucking daddy.

Chapter 9

Calista

"Thanks for calling to give me the results." My voice came out soft and shaky, the complete opposite of how I usually spoke. My normal confidence had been replaced by nerves that just wouldn't quit. When I made the decision to move to Atlanta, I knew my life was going to change—I just hadn't been prepared for quite how much it did. Even with all of Xander's talk about getting me pregnant over the last couple weeks, I hadn't expected it to actually happen. Not even after the urine test came back positive. But there was no doubting it anymore; I was pregnant with Xander's baby.

"Us," my baby daddy—holy shit, there was a phrase I never expected to be able to use—corrected as I disconnected from the call.

"Hmm?" I asked dazedly, sinking onto the plush cushions of the couch when my knees felt like they were going to give out. It was a new one that had turned up in the living room the day after I moved into Xander's house. I'd complained about his furniture choices since everything was black leather and chrome. The next thing I knew, it was all hauled away and replaced with new furnishings that worked well with all my stuff.

I still had no idea how he'd known what my things looked like since the truck didn't arrive until a few days after the new furniture he'd ordered. He'd refused to tell me when I'd asked, offering me a mysterious smile instead. Whatever stunt he'd pulled, it worked out well for me because I loved the new stuff he bought. But it did make me wonder what else he had up his sleeve.

"You told the doctor's office thank you for calling to give you the results—but you should have said us instead because I'm in this as much as you are."

I narrowed my eyes at him. "Umm, no. I'm the one who's going to gain all the weight, get poked and prodded at all the doctor's appointments, and will go through labor and delivery."

"But I'll be with you every step of the way." He dropped down to his knees in front of me and pressed a gentle kiss to my belly. "With the way you're talking, I'm assuming it's official? The blood test was positive, too?"

"Yeah." I smiled softly at him. It was hard to stay irritated with him when he was being so damn sweet. Or at least it was when I was pumped full of pregnancy hormones. The next eight and a half months were bound to be interesting.

"Fuck yeah!" he whooped, jumping to his feet and lifting me off the couch and into the air.

"Shit," I hissed, feeling lightheaded as he twirled me around.

"What?" he set me on my feet gently, his dark eyes filled with concern. "What is it?"

I plopped back onto the couch and tucked my head between my knees to make the room stop spinning. "No more picking me up like that."

"Fuck, baby," he sighed, rubbing my back in soft circles. "I'm sorry. I was so excited; I didn't even think. I promise I'll be more careful with you and our little dude from now on."

"Little dude?" I groaned. "Please tell me you're not going to be one of those guys who wants a son to carry on his father's name but hasn't even considered that he might have a daughter instead."

"Of course I've thought about having a daughter with you," he assured me. "A little girl with eyes so dark they almost look black at times. But then I also thought about what would happen when she grew up, and boys came around. Unless you want to see me carted off to jail for killing the first boy who breaks her heart, you'd better have a baby boy instead. Carrying on my name is only one of the advantages to having a boy, being around for our children's whole lives is what it's really all about."

"Your name," I whispered to myself. "Whole lives."

It finally struck me, exactly why he'd called himself my fiancé back at the doctor's office. I'd been too distracted by her announcement of the urine test results to put too much thought into it at that moment, but Xander seemed damn confident that I was going to marry him, give him more babies and spend the rest of my life with him. He talked about it like it was a foregone conclusion, but if he knew me better he might realize it wasn't what he wanted—even if it was a little too late to be thinking like that since I was already pregnant. Having a former CIA operative who'd done the things I had in the line of duty as his baby momma was a fuck of a lot different than having her for his wife and the mother of all his children. If I were a better woman, I would have come clean to him about the things which wouldn't get me arrested for sharing. But I hadn't been able to bring myself to do it, yet.

"Of course he'll have my name. So will you."

I cautiously raised my head and looked down at my hand to make sure he hadn't slipped an engagement ring onto my finger while I was napping. With as sneaky as he'd been about redecorating this place, I wouldn't have been too surprised. But there wasn't anything different to see, which meant he'd skipped a step. I lifted my hand up and wagged my fingers at him. "I think you forgot something—like a ring and a question I haven't answered yet."

"If you're feeling good enough to be sassy with me, then I guess you're up to a quick trip to the office."

"What kind of an answer is that?" I grumbled to myself as he gripped my hand and pulled me off the couch.

"The only kind you're getting for now." He led me through the kitchen and out to the garage.

"If I weren't pregnant, I'd kick your bossy ass."

"I do love when you call me boss, in whatever form you use." He helped me get settled into the passenger seat of his car. "But if you weren't pregnant, I'd let you try."

"I wouldn't be trying; I'd be doing."

"You hold onto that thought for the next ten or so months, and then you can challenge me as much as you want," he chuckled. "At least until I knock you up again."

"You're a cocky son of a bitch. I'll give you that."

"You've got that backwards, baby. *I'm* giving *you* my cock."

Startled laughter burst past my lips, and I shook my head at his antics. He was impossible, even more so now that he knew I was pregnant. I should have expected what he did when we walked into the Gray Security offices, but the pregnancy news had me off my usual stride.

"I need everybody out here!" he boomed as we walked through the glass doors. Poor Jessa almost fell out of her chair in surprise, while her grandmother merely laughed. Margaret had been back for about a week, but her efforts to train her granddaughter had been useless so far because Jessa was too intimidated by the guys to relax enough to learn what needed to be done.

About a half dozen people flowed out of offices and the gym to wander in our direction with questioning looks on their faces. Once they were all standing in front of us, Xander flung his arm over my shoulder and pulled me into his side.

"I know the gossip mill has been running full force since Calista started here. I haven't put a stop to it"—he gave me a tight squeeze as he looked at me apologetically—"because I didn't give a damn who knew about us. Calista wanted you all to judge her for her abilities and not her connection to me, but I think she's more than proven herself around here. Even if she hadn't, it would be tough shit because the news we received today means her role here is changing effective immediately."

"Oh, shit," I mumbled, knowing exactly where he was going with this. It wasn't a sky writer, but it sure as hell was just about as effective as one when it came to spreading the word about us.

"Changing how?" Chad, a guy who'd made it clear he thought I wasn't qualified to provide personal protection to Ewan, asked. I hadn't bothered Xander about it because it was my battle to fight, but I had a feeling that was going to change with this announcement.

"Calista is pregnant. With my baby," he added as if it wasn't already obvious to everyone in the room. "And she's going to take a backseat on cases from now on, lending her expertise in other ways."

"What other ways?" Chad's gaze darted between the two of us as he realized the shit he'd pulled with me might have put his job at risk, but that didn't stop him from speaking up.

"She's my second in command from here on out. If I'm not available, you go to her."

"She's done a decent job with the McKendry case, but that doesn't mean she's qualified to lead us."

"Are you fucking kidding me?" Xander scoffed. "I told you guys she was former CIA when I hired her. She has the qualifications and then some."

"As what? An analyst or something."

My spine straightened at that. It wasn't that I had anything against analysts, but I'd busted my ass in the CIA and saw more action than this guy ever had. I'd more than proven myself.

"She was not a fucking analyst," Xander growled. "None of you have seen her official file. But, I've seen the un-redacted version of her record, and trust me, she's more capable than any of you."

"You've what?" I gasped, as a mixture of shock and relief hit me. It didn't make sense, considering the clearance level of most of my missions. It shouldn't even be a possibility, but I found myself filled with hope anyway. If what he was saying was true, then it meant he wanted me even though he knew about my past with the CIA.

Chapter 10

Xander

Maybe I should have told her about my clearance before blurting it out to our entire staff. I honestly hadn't thought much about it; her file was catalogued in the "employee" part of my brain because it was only applicable to the job.

From the look on her face, it was clear that I'd mishandled the situation. I'd deal with that in a minute, though.

My eyes locked on Chad and I scowled at the condescending glare he was giving Calista. "Chad, I think you and I need to have a discussion. Be in my office at nine AM tomorrow." His expression slipped long enough to show a moment of indecision, obviously reconsidering his choice to speak up. He quickly covered it back up, nodded and spun around, striding down the hall toward the gym.

"Unless anyone else feels the need to

question my decisions..." I let the comment hang for a moment, waiting. No one spoke up, so I continued, "Over the next couple of weeks, we'll be scheduling time for each of you to meet with Calista so she can get to know you, after which you will have time with her in the gym, and she will assess your physical abilities. I want her to be as familiar with each of you as I am." Everyone else seemed to take the news like a professional with nods and murmurs of agreement. "All right, back to work." The crowd dispersed quickly, and I used the arm I had around Calista's shoulders to steer her to my office.

Once inside, I shut the door before walking us around to my desk chair, sitting and settling her on my lap.

"What did you mean when you said you'd read my entire file, even the redacted sections? Were you exaggerating to squash more dissension?" She sounded wary and pissed at the same time.

"Baby, you know I wouldn't lie to you, my employees, or anyone else." I felt like a pansy, but I wasn't able to keep the hurt out of my tone. "I do a lot of freelance work for the government, and I have code word clearance and am rarely denied access to the information I request. I didn't think to mention it because it had no bearing on our personal lives and, as an employee, it's my prerogative as the boss. After you left that first day, I read C. Lewis's whole file. But I did it as the CEO of Gray Security, not Xander Gray who was in love with Calista Lewis."

Calista gasped and leaned back so she could stare directly into my eyes. "In love?"

I laughed and kissed her nose, forehead, eyelids, and finally her mouth. "You think I'd knock up and demand to marry just any woman? For fuck's sale, baby. Of course I'm in love with you."

Her mouth had formed a little O, and her eyes were blinking owlishly. I decided to take advantage of the moment and opened the top right desk drawer. After locating the little box I was searching for, I opened it and removed a three-karat diamond ring. "About that question and a ring," I drawled. "There is no question, because we're getting married and that's final. However"—I softly kissed her lips as I slipped the ring onto the third finger of her left hand—"I do have a ring."

She studied me for a moment. "Since you've been doing your best to put your kid in me since the moment we met, I think I can safely assume that this proposal isn't because of the pregnancy?"

The tilt of her lips made me smile, and I laughed again. "That's just a perk, baby. You want to tell me why you're marrying me?"

Her dark eyes sparkled with mischief. "Who says I'm marrying you? I don't recall you asking," she sassed.

"You're marrying me," I growled. "This isn't up for debate. Now, tell me what I want to hear, baby."

"Yes."

I raised an eyebrow. "Yes, what?"

"Yes, I'll marry you."

Rolling my eyes, I twisted her around to straddle me and cupped her face in my hands. "Calista," I grunted, my voice full of warning. "Your pretty little ass is going to be cherry red soon if you don't stop being so cheeky."

"Cheeky?" Calista bubbled with laughter, and I lost myself in the beautiful sound. I fucking loved hearing her laugh.

But, it didn't distract me from my ultimate goal. I gripped the back of her head with one hand and used the other to land a quick smack on one ass cheek. "Woman, I am—"

"I love you."

"It's about fucking time," I growled before

crushing my lips down on hers.

I made good use of my sturdy desk to celebrate being officially engaged, then cleaned us both up before we headed back home.

As we passed by her desk, I gave Jessa a warm smile. "Great work today, Jessa. Goodnight."

She looked shocked, but she didn't jump and squeak. She simply gave me a wave back.

Calista laughed as we got on the elevator. "You're going to make that girl's head spin with your mood changes. Perhaps you should think about always being that nice to her."

"If it makes you happy." I shrugged. "When you're happy, I'm happy."

The elevator doors swooshed open to the lobby, and I clasped her hand in mine with a contented sigh as we exited the building.

At the sound of a shot, my world turned to slow motion. I pulled my gun and aimed in the direction the sound had appeared to come from, even as I moved to block Calista, but I felt like I was trying to swim through molasses. I couldn't get my sights on the shooter and focused on covering Calista. But she was already stumbling back, and I grabbed her arms to steady her. Her face was a mask of pain and... rage? Everything sped up to warp speed as she whipped out her gun and leaned around me and fired. People were screaming and running, but my sole focus was on Calista.

"Fuck!" she shouted in agony and frustration as her arm went limp. "I am so fucking sick of getting shot!" Her tone was furious, and if I hadn't been so fucking scared, I might have smiled at my woman's strength and how damn adorable she was. I searched for her wound and almost sighed with relief when I saw the red blood soaking the shoulder of her shirt. Tearing the fabric, I confirmed that it was superficial, but she'd fired with the injured arm and was clearly in a lot of pain as the adrenaline wore off.

"Shit, Calista, nice shot," Quinn said with awe as he jogged up to us. "Hit her in the fucking wrist just below her weapon."

"Who the fuck was shooting at her?" I bellowed.

Police cars and an ambulance came screeching to a stop across the street in front of a large park. Two more Gray Security employees had a mousy, brown haired woman in their grasp. She was screaming and crying as they hauled her to the ambulance and got her inside, two of the cops jumping in to escort her. Another ambulance pulled up in front of us, blocking our view of the drama unfolding across from us.

"Seriously?" Calista sighed. "You called the paramedics?"

"You were fucking shot, Calista," I barked. While Quinn shrugged and said, "Protocol."

They whisked us to the hospital where it was confirmed that the bullet had only left a shallow wound, not even deep enough for it to have gotten lodged in her shoulder. I made them check her everywhere and do an ultrasound, just to make sure both she and the baby were truly all right before I would even hear any talk of going home.

Calista didn't seem to care about the pain, the wound, anything, except how fucking mad she was that she'd been shot AGAIN in the same year, and even after leaving the CIA. Her tantrum was the cutest thing I'd ever seen, and I did my best to keep the smile off of my face, but she glared at me every time I failed.

"Knock it off, Gray," she snapped. "I swear, this is becoming a habit. The next time I get shot at, I'm not going to be so nice with my aim."

"Next time?" I shouted. "You will not be putting yourself in any situation where that is even a remote possibility. Is that clear?" She was about to answer when a young woman in a police uniform knocked on the door jam, requesting entrance.

"What can we do for you, Lieutenant Jensen?" I asked, reading her name tag.

"We checked your records and as you have a concealed carry permit, and witnesses recounted that she fired the first shot, no charges are being brought against you. The young woman is going to be fine. She'll likely lose a lot of the functions in her right hand, but it means it's unlikely that she'll ever hold a gun in it again. So, nice shot, Ms. Lewis." She glanced behind her before whispering, "Don't tell anyone I said that."

Calista laughed, but I wasn't in the mood for the cop's brevity. "Why was she shooting at my fiancée?"

She raised an eyebrow at the title, but I didn't comment, only continued to glare. "Oh, apparently she's the woman who's been stalking Ms. Lewis's boy—uh"—she shuffled uncomfortably—"stalking Ewan McKendry. She was screaming and mumbling to herself about a myriad of things, including talking about taking out the competition for Ewan. It's very likely she'll be serving out her sentence in a mental health facility."

She asked a few more questions then set a time for Calista to go down to the station the next day to give her statement. Shortly after, the doctor brought the test results, clearing Calista to go home.

I ordered dinner, and we picked it up on the way. Then I got her settled on the couch, made her take some Tylenol, and brought her food. Taking a seat on the opposite end of the couch, I lifted her feet into my lap and simply watched her. I'd set my food on the coffee table, but it remained untouched, I had no appetite.

"Baby," I murmured and waited until she looked at me. "I can't go through this again. You know I want you to do what makes you happy, but fuck, I think I'm going to have to put my foot down on this. No more field work. I can't imagine my life without you, and I'd spend every day as a nervous wreck. It will put me in an early grave."

She sat up and set her food on the small table as well, then crawled across the couch and into my arms. "No need for you to go all caveman, honey. I'd already made that decision when I left your office with your ring on my finger. I'm going to be a wife and mother; those things trump everything else. I don't want to quit and helping you run the business intrigues me."

I gathered her up even closer in my arms, careful of her shoulder, and kissed the crown of her head, inhaling the sweet fragrance of her silky hair. "I love you so fucking much, baby. I don't know how I lived the last thirty years without you."

"I love you too. And, I'm not sure how you survived without me either, I'm pretty fucking awesome."

I threw my head back and laughed before kissing the fuck out of her. "You're definitely a badass, baby. And it's hot as fuck."

She leaned in so her lips brushed the shell of my ear as she spoke. "Does that mean you get turned on when I threaten to kick your ass?"

"Fuck yeah."

She bit the lobe, and a shiver raced down my spine, all the blood in my body suddenly surging into my cock. "I can't kick your ass until the baby is born but... I'll let you tie me up," she breathed.

I didn't remember how we got to the bedroom, but I remembered every single fucking detail of what happened after.

Epilogue

Calista

The sight in front of me was beyond adorable. So much so, I could barely concentrate enough to record it with my phone. My gorgeous baby girl twirled across the dance floor in her purple leotard and pink tutu. Her long, brown hair was pulled into a ponytail that whipped back and forth, and her dark eyes were lit up with laughter. She was always happy when she danced, but she was on could nine this time around because of the tall, dark-haired man following behind her. His hair was tousled as usual, and I could see the outline of his nipple rings through the purple T-shirt that clung to his sculpted chest, one our baby girl had picked out so she and her daddy matched. The shirt hid all his tattoos, including the two names inked right over his heart—our baby girl's, Madison, and mine. He had them done the week after she was born.

He was hotter than ever, even while failing miserably at the dance moves he was supposed to be doing. Not that any of the moms in the audience seemed to mind. When I'd signed him up to participate in the Daddy & Daughters special event at the school where she took her dancing classes, Madison's teacher had told me it would fill up quickly once word got out. Judging by the lack of empty chairs, it looked like she was right. I couldn't blame them, though.

My husband was damn fine eye candy—extremely loyal man candy at that since he never seemed to notice the flirtatious glances so many women sent his way. I noticed each and every one, but I didn't let them get to me since I knew that if any of them were stupid enough to try to get too close to him, I could easily kick their asses. I was a mommy, but that didn't mean I didn't keep up with my fighting skills once I'd received the clearance from my doctor. And the first place I'd put them to use was a no-holds-barred spar with Chad, where I'd pounded his ass into the mat. Whatever Xander had said to them in their meeting the morning after we'd found out I was pregnant had worked because his attitude made a complete turnaround. But that didn't mean I'd forgotten the shit he'd pulled back when Xander and I first got together, and I made sure he knew it.

"Did you see us, Mommy?" Madison screamed as she ran towards me.

I knelt down to wrap my arms around her as she crashed into me. "I sure did, baby girl."

"Daddy and me danced so good togever." She turned to look up at him when he joined us. "Didn't we, Daddy?"

"You were amazing, Maddiekins."

I could almost hear ovaries exploding all around me. Mine would be, too, if I wasn't already pregnant again. When we found out Madison was a girl, Xander had sworn we couldn't have any more children because it would just up his odds of getting tossed in jail for killing teenage boys later in life. After her third birthday, he'd been bitten by the baby bug again. It had taken him less than a couple of weeks to knock me up, and he'd breathed a huge sigh of relief last week when the ultrasound had shown this one was a boy. Then he'd mumbled something about needing the extra backup since Madison was a handful like her mommy.

"You did kinda amazing, too, Daddy." She smiled up at him sweetly. "I'm sure you'll do better next time if we practice lots and lots."

"What an excellent idea, Madison. Daddy looked like he was having so much fun up there, I bet he wants to come to your classes to practice with you every day from now on."

"Yay!" she screeched before running to the side of the room to grab her dance bag.

"You're going to pay for that later," Xander growled, as if we both didn't know he'd have his ass right back on the dance floor any time Madison wanted him there.

"Oh, please," I laughed. "Like I don't know that I'm always safe with you."

And I was... even when he was making me pay at night for whatever hell I'd raised during the day.

Books By This Author

Risqué Contracts Series

Penalty Clause

Contingency Plan

Fraternization Rule

Yeah, Baby Series

Baby, You're Mine

Baby Steps

Baby, Don't Go

Dance With Me, Baby

I'm Yours, Baby

Brief Me, Baby

Play With Me, Baby

Mafia Ties: Nic & Anna

Deception

Danger

Devotion

Mafia Ties: Brandon & Carly

Pursuit

Power

Passion

Standalones

My Father's Best Friend

My Step-Dad's Brother

Not-So Temporarily Married

The One I Want For Christmas

Sex & Vows

Until Death Do We Part

For You, I Will

About the Author

The writing duo of Elle Christensen and Rochelle Paige team up under the Fiona Davenport pen name to bring you sexy, insta-love stories filled with alpha males. If you want a quick & dirty read with a guaranteed happily ever after, then give Fiona Davenport a try!

You can also connect with Fiona online on Facebook or Twitter.